Katie Morag's
Island Stories

To Isabella

July 2016

the taste of scotland

love Martha and Angus

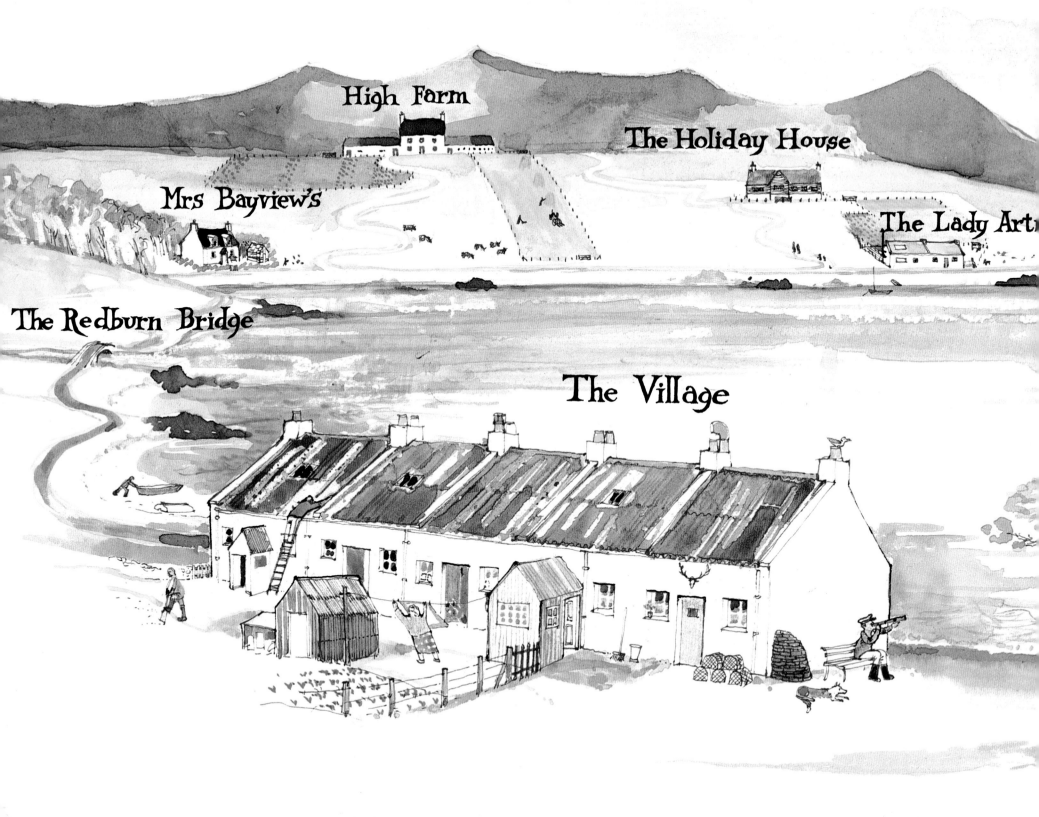

THE ISLE of STRUAY

Grannie's

The Mainland

ISLE of STRUAY
SHOP & POST OFFICE

OBAN TIMES
GET YOUR COPY HERE

The Jetty

The Shop & Post Office

KATIE MORAG'S ISLAND STORIES

A RED FOX BOOK

978 1 849 41088 5

First published in Great Britain by The Bodley Head,
an imprint of Random House Children's Publishers UK
A Random House Group Company

The Bodley Head edition published 1995
Red Fox edition published 2003
This Red Fox edition published 2010

Copyright © Mairi Hedderwick, 1995

Originally published as individual editions:

Katie Morag Delivers the Mail
First published in Great Britain by The Bodley Head in 1984,
copyright © Mairi Hedderwick 1984

Katie Morag and the Two Grandmothers
First published in Great Britain by The Bodley Head in 1985,
copyright © Mairi Hedderwick 1985

Katie Morag and the Tiresome Ted
First published in Great Britain by The Bodley Head in 1986,
copyright © Mairi Hedderwick 1986

Katie Morag and the Big Boy Cousins
First published in Great Britain by The Bodley Head in 1987,
copyright © Mairi Hedderwick 1987

10

Red Fox Books are published by Random House Children's Publishers UK,
61–63 Uxbridge Road, London W5 5SA

www.**randomhousechildrens**.co.uk

Addresses for companies within The Random House Group Limited can be found at: www.randomhouse.co.uk/offices.htm

THE RANDOM HOUSE GROUP Limited Reg. No. 954009

A CIP catalogue record for this book is available from the British Library

Printed in China

Katie Morag
Island Stories

Mairi Hedderwick

RED FOX

KATIE MORAG
DELIVERS THE MAIL

Wednesdays were always hectic on the Isle of Struay, for that was the day that the boat brought mail and provisions from the mainland.

One particular Wednesday was worse than usual, since baby Liam was cutting his first tooth and both Mr and Mrs McColl were in a bad mood.

"All right, all right," said Mrs McColl in exasperation. "I'll take Liam upstairs to quieten him down! Katie Morag, you take the mail to the houses across the Bay. There are five parcels – one for each house. The one with the red label is for Grannie."

Pleased to escape, Katie Morag set off. She loved any excuse to visit her Grannie, who lived all alone in the very last house on the other side of the Bay.

But it was a hot day, and Katie Morag had just stopped for a moment to paddle in a pool beneath the Redburn Bridge, when suddenly – *splash!* – she slipped on a slithery stone and fell into the water, mailbag and all.

"Oh, dear! Oh, dear!" wailed Katie Morag looking at the five soggy parcels. "All the addresses are smudged and I won't know which parcel is for which house now!"

Only Grannie's parcel was still recognizable by its red label.

Then, because she was so frightened and ashamed, Katie Morag did a silly thing. She ran the rest of the way to the other side of the Bay and threw a

parcel – any parcel, except the red-labelled one – on to the doorstep of each of the first four houses. Nobody saw her. Still sobbing, she ran on to Grannie's.

"Well, this is a fine *boorach* you've got yourself into, Katie Morag," said Grannie, when Katie Morag had explained what she had done. "Still at least you've given *me* the right parcel – it's got the spare part for the tractor that I've been waiting for. I'll go and get the old grey lady going, while you dry yourself up. Then you can try and sort the whole muddle out."

Grannie had her head under the bonnet of the tractor for a long time.
Occasionally, Katie Morag heard muffled words of anger and she thought of
the angry words waiting for her at home…

Then, suddenly, with a cough of black smoke, the tractor stuttered into life
and they set off to go round each of the four houses in turn.

The first house belonged to the Lady Artist. She had been expecting tiny, thin brushes for her miniature paintings, but the parcel Katie Morag had left on her doorstep contained two enormous brushes.

"They're bigger than my painting boards!" she said in disgust.

The second house was rented by the Holiday People. They had ordered fishing hooks from a sports catalogue, but their parcel had been full of garden seeds.

"We can't catch fish with daisies and lettuces!" they complained.

At the third house, Mr MacMaster was standing by a big barrel of whitewash, holding the Lady Artist's paint brushes.
"How can I paint my walls with these fiddling little things?" he asked.

In the fourth house lived Mrs Bayview. "That stupid shop on the mainland!
Where are my seeds? Flowers won't grow out of *these*," she said crossly,
waving a packet of fishing hooks in the air.

After much trundling back and forth, Katie Morag finally managed to
collect and deliver all the right things to all the right people.
Everyone smiled and waved and said, "Thank you very much."

By now it was getting dark. Katie Morag thought of the long journey home. She would be very late and her parents were so bad-tempered these days on account of Liam's noisy teething.

"Grannie, would you like to come back for tea?" she asked.

Katie Morag half hid behind Grannie as they walked in the kitchen door but, to her surprise, everyone was smiling. Liam had cut his tooth at last and all was calm.

"Thank you for helping out today, Katie Morag," said Mrs McColl. "Isn't she good, Grannie?"

"Och aye," said Grannie with a smile as she looked at Katie Morag. "She's very good at sorting things out, is our Katie Morag." And she said no more.

Katie Morag and the Two Grandmothers

One sunny Wednesday morning Mrs McColl woke Katie Morag early.

"Hurry up, now!" she said, drawing back the curtains. "Here comes the boat. Granma Mainland will be here soon and you've still got this room to tidy for her."

Granma Mainland lived far away in the big city. She was coming to stay with them for a holiday.

Katie Morag went with her other grandmother, Grannie Island, who lived just across the Bay, to meet the boat.

"My, you're still a smart wee Bobby Dazzler," said Neilly Beag, as he helped Granma Mainland down.

Grannie Island revved the engine *very* loudly. BUROOM . . . BUROOM . . . BUROOM . . .

Katie Morag watched, fascinated, as Granma Mainland unpacked.

"Do you like this new hat I've brought for Show Day, Katie Morag?" Granma Mainland asked.

"Och, her and her fancy ways!" muttered Grannie Island to herself.

Show Day was always a big event on the Island of Struay. At the Post Office, Mr and Mrs McColl were rushed off their feet.

"*Look* where you're GOING!" shouted Mrs McColl, as Katie Morag tripped over baby Liam.

"Katie Morag, I think you'd be better off helping Grannie Island get Alecina ready for the Show," sighed Mr McColl.

Alecina was Grannie Island's prize sheep. She had won the Best Ewe and
Fleece Trophy for the past seven years, but she was getting old, and everyone
said that Neilly Beag's April Love would win it this year.

Pets' Corner

HOME PRODUCE HANDICRAFTS

Katie Morag ran as fast as she could, past the Show Field, where frantic last-minute preparations were in progress, and on to Grannie Island's in order to give Alecina an extra special brush and comb before the judging started.

But when Katie Morag arrived at Grannie Island's, Alecina was up to her horns in the Boggy Loch.

"A whole hillside to eat and she wants *that* blade of grass!" cried Grannie Island in a fury.

"Look at your fleece! And today of *all* days, you old devil!" ranted Grannie Island when they eventually got Alecina out of the Boggy Loch. "We'll never get these peaty stains out in time for the Show!"

"Granma Mainland has some stuff to make *her* hair silvery white ..." said Katie Morag thoughtfully.

Everyone looked in amazement as Grannie Island's old tractor and
trailer hurtled past the Show Field, heading for the Post Office.
"We'll be too late!" grumbled Grannie Island.

Fortunately, no one was about when they got home, since Mrs McColl
would certainly not have approved of this . . .

. . . or this.

And Granma Mainland would have been furious at this . . .

. . . not to mention this.

But all ended well. They managed to get tidied up and back to the Show Field just in time for the judging, and, at the sight of Alecina's shiny coat and curls, the judges were in no doubt as to who should win the Silver Trophy again this year.

That evening there was a party at Grannie Island's to celebrate.
"My, but thon old ewe is still some beauty for her age," said Neilly Beag.
"Just like yourself, Granma Mainland. How do you do it?"
"Ah, that's *my* secret," said wee Granma Mainland, fluttering her eyelashes.

Katie Morag and Grannie Island smiled at each other. They knew some of the secret, but would never tell.

And Grannie Island never frowned at Granma Mainland's "fancy ways" ever again. I wonder why?

KATIE MORAG AND THE TIRESOME TED

There was great excitement on the Isle of Struay. Mrs McColl at the Post Office had had a new baby, and everyone was delighted.

Everyone, that is, except Katie Morag. She had been in a bad mood ever since the new baby had arrived.

"No one talks to *me* any more," she grumbled to herself, "or brings *me* presents."

"Don't worry," everyone said knowingly. "Katie Morag will soon get over it."

But Katie Morag could not and would not get over it. She kept doing naughty things, like stamping her feet and nipping her little brother, Liam. One day she was so cross that she stomped all the way down to the jetty and kicked her friendly old one-eyed teddy bear into the sea.

"Tiresome Ted!" she shouted, as he disappeared into the choppy waves.

Mrs McColl was at her wit's end. "How can I cope with running the Post Office *and* with looking after the new baby *and* Liam, when Katie Morag is behaving like this?" she asked, throwing her arms up in despair.

Mr McColl said that he *was* trying to help.

Grannie Island picked up a basketful of the baby's dirty washing and left, saying they could send Katie Morag over to stay with her, if she became too much of a handful.

That night the first of the winter storms battered at the window. Katie Morag could not sleep. She wondered what had become of her old teddy and she began to wish she hadn't thrown him away.

She crept over to Liam's bed and took his hot-water bottle . . . but it didn't make her feel much better.

The next morning things seemed even worse. Katie Morag woke up to a wet bed. Liam thought it was very funny, but Mrs McColl was furious. It was the last straw.

"I think perhaps Katie Morag should go to Grannie Island's for a few days, after all," sighed Mr McColl.

Katie Morag trudged slowly over to Grannie Island's on the other side of the Bay.

"Having bad moods is very tiring," she thought to herself, and so engrossed was she with her own crossness that she didn't notice a familiar object being flung up by the waves of the incoming tide.

The bad weather lasted for two whole days and nights. Grannie Island could not get on with the washing, and Katie Morag was forced to stay indoors. She wondered how everyone was back at home.

And all the while her old teddy bear lay abandoned on the beach in front of Grannie Island's house. He was a sorry sight.

At last, the rain stopped and the sun came out. Katie Morag felt much better and she decided to stop being in a bad mood. She went down to the high tide-line to collect driftwood for Grannie's stove.

Katie Morag found all sorts of other interesting things that had been washed up by the storm: a ball for Liam, a box for Mr McColl, a bottle for Mrs McColl and a beautiful, big conch shell.

"I'll give this to the new baby," thought Katie Morag, "and show her how to hear the sea."

ALICE 086

It was only then that Katie Morag noticed the two furry arms sticking up through the seaweed. She couldn't believe her eyes. Old Ted wasn't lost, after all.

Katie Morag rushed back to Grannie's and dried her teddy out by the stove. She filled his tummy with some fluffy sheep's wool and then laboriously began sewing up the large tear in his tummy.

Buttons

But even with his new eye on, he still looked the worse for the wear. When Grannie Island wasn't looking, Katie Morag took something out of the washing-basket.

The journey back to the Post Office seemed to take ages. Katie Morag couldn't wait to get home to show everyone the things she had found down by the shore.

The other islanders were pleased to see Katie Morag looking like her old self again. "She's got over it," they all said, nodding their heads.

"Thank you for the lovely presents, Katie Morag," said Mrs McColl. "And thank you, Grannie Island, for doing all that washing."

"It's good to have our Katie Morag back, and to see Old Ted again," said Mr McColl, smiling.

"I'll never, ever throw him away again, or call him Tiresome Ted," said Katie Morag, and she meant it.

And nobody said a thing about the missing Babygro from Mrs McColl's washing-basket, which was perhaps just as well.

KATIE MORAG AND THE
BIG BOY COUSINS

It was the second fortnight in July, and Katie Morag's Big Boy Cousins had arrived from the Mainland to camp at Grannie Island's, as they did each summer.

"Oh, no!" sighed the islanders. "Here they come AGAIN!"
The Big Boy Cousins were very wild and unruly. Katie Morag thought they were wonderful.

"Why do you put up with them, Grannie Island?" exclaimed Mr and Mrs McColl.

"Because nobody else will have them!" declared Grannie Island. "And I could do with some help with the chores."

Grannie Island loaded the provisions into her tractor and trailer, ready for the long, bumpy journey back to her house on the other side of the Bay. "Coming, Katie Morag?" smiled the biggest Boy Cousin called Hector.

Soon the tent was pitched and the stores unloaded.

"Now," called Grannie Island. "There are potatoes to be dug up, peats to be fetched and driftwood to be gathered. Who is doing what?"

"GEE WHILICKERS!" groaned Hector, Archie, Jamie, Dougal and Murdo Iain.

Everyone pretended not to hear Grannie Island, even Katie Morag.

"Hide down by the shore!" whispered Hector.

"It's boring here," moaned Archie, after a while.

"We'll go to the Village, then, and play Chickenelly," said Hector.

"Yeah!" chorused all the Big Boy Cousins – except for Murdo Iain.

"It's an awful long walk," he whined.

"I know a quick way," chirped up Katie Morag.

She was enjoying being naughty and continued to ignore Grannie Island's cries for help.

In the Village all was calm and peaceful. The villagers were inside their houses, having a well-earned rest after a morning's hard work.

Nobody noticed Grannie Island's heavily laden boat, heading across the Bay.

Chickenelly was a daring game.

"Last one gets caught!" whispered Hector, as he led all the cousins on tiptoe round the gable end of Nurse's house.

Katie Morag's tummy tickled inside with excitement.

Then the Big Boy Cousins, with Katie Morag close on their heels, ran as fast as greased lightning, the length of the Village, banging very loudly on each back door.

BANG-a-BANG-a-BANG-a-BANG-a-BANG!

In their mad rush to get to the safety of the other end of the village houses, they knocked into all sorts of things, and nobody saw Grannie Island racing round the head of the Bay on her tractor.

"And just WHAT do you think you are all up to?" Grannie Island was colossal with fury.

"Chickenelly," said Katie Morag, timidly, wishing she had never heard of the game.

"Gee whilickers!" groaned Hector, Archie, Dougal, Jamie and Murdo Iain.

Grannie Island made them all apologize to the upset villagers and told them to clear up the mess they had caused.

"And you can all WALK back when you are finished!" she shouted.

Even though Grannie Island was angry outside, Katie Morag knew her Grannie was sad inside, and that made Katie Morag feel sad, too.

Tired and very hungry, the Big Boy Cousins were silent on the long journey back to Grannie Island's.
Katie Morag walked as fast as she could.

"We've got to say sorry to Grannie," she said.
"*And* help her with the chores."
"Gee whilickers!" groaned Hector, Archie, Dougal, Jamie *and* Murdo Iain.

The chores didn't take that long once everyone lent a hand. Katie Morag worked hardest of them all, and she made sure that the Big Boy Cousins didn't skive.

"Last chore!" called a smiling Grannie Island. "Bring over some of the potatoes, the peats and the driftwood."

Nobody groaned "Gee whilickers" this time. Grannie Island had made a barbecue.

"This is what I would call a hard-earned feast," said Grannie Island, dishing out mounds of fried tatties and beans.

"Tomorrow – " she continued – "*after* the chores, we'll go fishing and see what we can catch for another feast."

"*Not* chickenellies!" giggled Katie Morag.

And when it came to toasting the marshmallows, Katie Morag made sure Grannie Island got the biggest one.

That was fair, wasn't it?

Join Katie Morag on more adventures!